D1445446

Strawberry Shortcake
Goes to School

Grosset & Dunlap

Published by Grosset & Dunlap, a division of Penguin Young Readers Group,
345 Hudson Street, New York, NY 10014. GROSSET & DUNLAP is a trademark of
Penguin Group (USA) Inc. Published simultaneously in Canada. Printed in China.

ISBN 0-448-43188-2   A B C D E F G H I J

Special Markets ISBN 0-448-43707-4

Strawberry Shortcake
Goes to School

By Emily Sollinger
Illustrated by SI Artists

Grosset & Dunlap • New York

"Today is the first day of school,"
Strawberry Shortcake told her pets Custard
and Pupcake. "I am *berry* excited. I can't wait
to see my classroom, and meet the kids in my class.

"What should I wear to school?" Strawberry wondered aloud.

"How should I know?" Custard grumbled sleepily. "Cats don't go to school!"

"Oh, Custard! You are so silly." Strawberry giggled. "*I know!* I will wear my favorite jeans and my striped shirt. And I'll bring my red sweatshirt."

Strawberry quickly got dressed.

Then she packed her backpack. "I think I will bring a pencil and paper and my box of crayons for coloring," she said.

"I will bring my lunch to school in my brand-new lunchbox," Strawberry told Custard and Pupcake.

Strawberry made a peanut butter and strawberry jelly sandwich. She packed a bag full of strawberries. She wrapped up two strawberry-chip cookies. Then she placed a box of strawberry juice in her lunchbox. *Yum!*

Strawberry Shortcake looked at the clock. "Oh, no! School starts in ten minutes. I'd better hurry up or I'll be late!" She grabbed her backpack and dashed out the door.

"Good-bye, Custard and Pupcake. I'll be back after school, okay?"

"I wish we could come with you," said Custard.

"I'll be back before you know it! I promise," Strawberry said.

Strawberry walked quickly. Finally, she saw her school. Wow! It looks so big, she thought to herself. Who will I play with? Who will I sit with at lunch? Strawberry felt a little scared.

Strawberry was glad to see her friends at school.

"Hi, Orange Blossom and Huckleberry Pie! Hello, Angel Cake! I'm so glad to see you, Ginger Snap!" she called. "I thought I wouldn't know any kids in my class!"

"We're glad to see you, too, Strawberry!" her friends answered.

"Look, Strawberry! Everyone in the class has their own cubby," said Huckleberry Pie excitedly.

"*Berry* cool!" Strawberry replied. She found her cubby and put her backpack and sweatshirt inside.

"Come on, Strawberry!" said Huck. "Put your lunch away and come sit next to me."

My lunch? Uh-oh! Where is my lunchbox? Strawberry wondered. It wasn't in her backpack. It wasn't under her sweatshirt. It wasn't on the floor. *Oh, no! I left my lunch at home.*

What would Strawberry do? There wasn't enough time for her to go home to get her lunch. School had already started.

When the kids sang the alphabet song, Strawberry didn't sing loud like everybody else. She didn't feel like it. She was sad about her lunch. *I'm already hungry! What will I do when it's lunchtime and I have nothing to eat?* she wondered.

Next, it was time for counting. The kids counted their numbers from one to ten.

But Strawberry didn't want to count her numbers. She was still worried about lunchtime.

At lunchtime, all of the kids rushed to their cubbies—
but not Strawberry.

"I made a peanut butter and huckleberry jam sandwich.
I can't wait to eat it!" Huck told his friends.

"I made special cookies in the shape of crayons!"
exclaimed Ginger Snap.

"What did you bring, Strawberry?" asked Orange Blossom.

"Nothing," Strawberry told her friends sadly. "I forgot my lunch at home."

She began to cry.

"Don't cry, Strawberry Shortcake,"
Orange Blossom said.
    "But what will I eat for lunch?"
asked Strawberry Shortcake sadly.

Angel Cake had an idea. "Strawberry, you can have some of my lunch, if you want."

"I will share my lunch with you, too!" offered Orange Blossom.

"Me too!" said Ginger Snap.

"Wow, that's *berry* nice of you. What *berry* kind friends you are!" Strawberry Shortcake said.

Ginger Snap gave Strawberry Shortcake a delicious crayon-shaped cookie decorated with frosting and sparkly sprinkles.

Orange Blossom poured some orange juice
into a cup for Strawberry.

Angel Cake gave Strawberry Shortcake a tiny strawberry shortcake with lots of whipped cream. *Yum!* Strawberry shortcake is Strawberry Shortcake's favorite dessert!

"Huck, what do you have?" asked Ginger Snap.

"W–well, I only have one sandwich." Huck replied quietly. "And *I* want to eat it."

"But Huck, sharing doesn't mean that you have to give away *all* of your sandwich—just part of it! When friends share, *everyone* gets something!" explained Orange Blossom.

Huck thought for a minute. Then he broke his sandwich in half and gave it to Strawberry. "Here you go, Strawberry! I hope you like huckleberry jam."

"Thanks, Huck! Thanks, *everybody!* This lunch is delicious!"

Just then, Custard and Pupcake arrived. "Strawberry, you left your lunch at home! We were so worried that you wouldn't have anything to eat." Custard said excitedly, barely taking a breath. Pupcake wagged his tail.

"Wow! Thank you, Custard and Pupcake! Now I can share the lunch that I made with *everyone*!" Strawberry exclaimed.

But when Strawberry opened her lunchbox, it was empty! "You silly dog!" shouted Custard. "I told you to carry Strawberry's lunch, not eat it!"

"It's okay, Pupcake. Lucky for me, my berry best friends shared their lunches!" Strawberry told her dog.

After lunch, it was time for recess!
Strawberry and her friends had lots
of fun on the playground.

After recess, Custard and Pupcake headed home,
and the kids went back inside the classroom.
They were tired after so much running around.
Luckily, it was rest time.

The first day of school was over. It was time to go home. It had been a great day!

"School is *berry* cool! See you tomorrow, everybody. And I promise I won't forget my lunch!"